First American Edition.

Published in the United States by Grolier Enterprises Inc., Danbury, Connecticut. Originally published in Denmark by Egmont Gruppen, Copenhagen.

ISBN: 0-7172-8812-9

Manufactured in the United States of America.
A B C D 1 2 3 4

Disney's

101 DALMATIANS

Treasure Hunters

GROLIER
BOOK CLUB EDITION

“Oh, Roger,” said Anita one afternoon. “I’m so happy here in our new country home! I can tell that our Dalmatians are much happier here, too.”

Roger smiled at his wife. “Yes, it is nice to have all this room for them to play,” he answered.

Nanny frowned. "I wish they would play somewhere else. The flower bed is full of holes."

It was true. The puppies just loved to dig in the soft, fragrant dirt!

That night, Anita called Roger and Nanny into the living room. The puppies were watching a television show called *Young Treasure Hunters*.

"No wonder the puppies are digging so much!" Nanny grumbled. "This show is all about digging for treasure!"

Roger turned off the television. "No more *Young Treasure Hunters*!" he scolded. "And from now on, no more digging in the garden."

Pongo and Perdita tried to explain that digging in the garden was naughty. "Our pets want to enter their garden in a contest," explained Perdita.

"But they won't be able to do that if you keep digging," added Pongo.

The puppies promised to try not to dig any more holes.

The next day, Roger and Anita got to work filling in the holes. When they had finished, Anita said, “Well, I hope the puppies have learned their lesson!”

But the next morning, the yard was full of holes once more. The puppies had been at it again!

Roger was very upset. “We’ll never be able to enter our garden in the contest,” he complained. Then he had an idea.

Roger began building a special pen for the puppies. “This will keep them out of the garden,” he told Anita.

“But…” Anita began.

“No buts. The puppies will stay in here until the contest is over,” Roger said firmly.

When the pen was finished, Pongo and Perdita watched as their puppies slowly walked inside. They felt as downhearted as the puppies.

The puppies were very sorry they had dug all those holes. They didn't want to stay in the pen.

"Oh, Roger," said Anita, "they look so sad."

Roger sighed. "Perhaps we shouldn't enter the garden contest, after all."

Then Nanny had an idea. “Why don’t I take the puppies out to the meadow every morning?” Nanny said. “They can dig as much as they like *there,* and when we come back they’ll be too tired to dig *here*.”

Everyone thought that was a splendid idea.

Nanny was up bright and early the next morning. "I hope this plan works," she said to herself.

"Good morning, puppies!" Nanny said when she opened the gate. The puppies were happy to see her and ran out of the pen.

Pongo and Perdita joined Nanny and the puppies. Soon they were all enjoying the bright sunshine in the meadow. The puppies ran and played. And no one minded their digging one bit!

“Nanny is almost as
clever as a Dalmatian,”
Pongo said to Perdita.

“What could be beyond those trees?” Nanny wondered.

"We may find a river..."

"...or a lake..."

"...or maybe even a mountain!"

"Or even treasure!" thought Lucky.

But the only thing on the other side of the trees was a big hole! It was part of an old gravel pit.

"Whoever dug that hole must be in *big* trouble!" Lucky said to his brothers and sisters.

They all turned to go. Just then, Lucky began to bark. "What's wrong, Lucky?" asked Nanny. "It's just an old gravel pit. There's nothing here."

Lucky grabbed the bottom of Nanny's dress.
"Lucky! Let go! It's time to go home!" she cried.
But Lucky wouldn't let go until Nanny looked into the hole again.

Suddenly, Nanny saw what Lucky was so excited about. "What on earth can that be?" she said, looking into the deep hole. "We must take a closer look."

Nanny and the puppies hurried down the slope for a better look. "Oh, isn't this exciting!" Nanny cried. "It's as if we're on our very own treasure hunt!"

Sure enough, there was a huge bone sticking up out of the dirt. The puppies began to sniff and bark.

Nanny found a shovel and began to dig. "Dig!" she called to the puppies. "Maybe we can find other bones!"

Together, they found a lot of bones. “Let’s put them in a safe place,” said Nanny. “We can come back tomorrow and dig for more. This evening, I’ll go to the library and look for a book on bones.”

Meanwhile, Roger and Anita were busy working in their garden once more.

"I hope Nanny's plan works," said Roger.

"I hope so, too," said Anita. "But it isn't easy to tire out 99 puppies."

But Nanny's plan did work!

When the puppies got home, they fell asleep at once—and so did Nanny.

"Nanny is a genius," Roger told Anita. "Those puppies are too tired even to think about digging holes in the garden."

The next morning, Nanny and her treasure hunters set out once more.

"This book should tell us more about those bones we found," Nanny said. "I think we've found something very special."

Back at home, Roger was taking the puppy pen apart.

"We won't be needing this, after all," he told Anita.

"Good old Nanny," Anita said. "Thanks to her, we have our garden back."

Every day, Nanny and the puppies dug up more bones. Soon they had a very big pile.

"I must write to the scientist who wrote that book," Nanny said. "Surely he will want to hear about all those bones."

Anita was busy writing, too. She was writing an essay for the garden contest.

"Do you think we will win a prize?" she asked Roger. "There are so many lovely gardens in the country."

But Roger didn't answer. He was busy writing a new song.

Back in the city, the scientist was very excited by Nanny's letter. He came to see the bones right away.

"Amazing!" he cried when he saw them. "How did you find these bones?"

"Lucky found the first bone. The other puppies helped find the rest," Nanny explained.

Nanny and the scientist carefully placed the bones in the scientist's truck. The puppies helped, too.

Pongo was very proud of the puppies as he watched them load the truck.

That very afternoon, Anita and Roger won a prize in the garden contest.

"What well-behaved puppies you have!" said the judge. "Not a single hole to be seen."

A few days later, Nanny received an important letter.

"Why, Nanny!" Anita cried as she read it. "It's an invitation to the museum! And the puppies are invited, too!"

Roger and Anita were very excited when they found out what Nanny and the puppies had been up to. They all went to the museum together.

A crowd of people stood around a big dinosaur skeleton.

"I thought that's what all those bones were going to make!" said Nanny.

Then the mayor began speaking. "We would like to thank Nanny and all the Dalmatians for finding this wonderful treasure," he began.

The puppies wagged their tails. They couldn't wait to begin digging for new treasure!